Dear Parent:

Your child's love of reading starts here!

Every child learns to read in a different way and at his or her own speed. You can help your young reader improve and become more confident by encouraging his or her own interests and abilities. You can also guide your child's spiritual development by reading stories with biblical values and Bible stories, like I Can Read! books published by Zonderkidz. From books your child reads with you to the first books he or she reads alone, there are I Can Read! books for every stage of reading:

SHARED READING
Basic language, word repetition, and whimsical illustrations, ideal for sharing with your emergent reader.

BEGINNING READING
Short sentences, familiar words, and simple concepts for children eager to read on their own.

READING WITH HELP
Engaging stories, longer sentences, and language play for developing readers.

READING ALONE
Complex plots, challenging vocabulary, and high-interest topics for the independent reader.

ADVANCED READING
Short paragraphs, chapters, and exciting themes for the perfect bridge to chapter books.

I Can Read! books have introduced children to the joy of reading since 1957. Featuring award-winning authors and illustrators and a fabulous cast of beloved characters, I Can Read! books set the standard for beginning readers.

A lifetime of discovery begins with the magical words **"I Can Read!"**

Visit <u>www.icanread.com</u> for information on enriching your child's reading experience.
Visit <u>www.zonderkidz.com</u> for more Zonderkidz I Can Read! titles.

Be joyful together with God's people.
—Deuteronomy 32:43

Happy Birthday Barnabas
Copyright © 2008 by Amaze Entertainment, Inc.
Illustrations copyright © 2008 by Amaze Entertainment, Inc.

Requests for information should be addressed to:
Zonderkidz, Grand Rapids, Michigan 49530

Library of Congress Cataloging-in-Publication Data

Lepp, Royden, 1980-
      Happy birthday, Barnabas / story by Royden Lepp ; pictures by Royden Lepp.
          p. cm. – (I can read! My first)
      Summary: Barnabas Bear thanks Jesus when his friends in Brookdale Wood throw him
      a surprise birthday party.
      ISBN-13: 978-0-310-71586-3 (softcover)
      ISBN-10: 0-310-71586-5 (softcover)
      [1. Birthdays–Fiction. 2. Parties–Fiction. 3. Bears–Fiction. 4. Animals–Fiction.
5. Christian life–Fiction.] I. Title.
PZ7.L5557Hap 2008
[E]–dc22

                                           2007023105

All Scripture quotations, unless otherwise indicated, are taken from the HOLY BIBLE,
NEW INTERNATIONAL READER'S VERSION®. Copyright © 1995, 1996, 1998 by
International Bible Society. Used by permission of Zondervan. All Rights Reserved.

Art Direction: Jody Langley
Cover Design: Sarah Molegraaf

Printed in China

---

08 09 10 • 4 3 2 1

Happy Birthday Barnabas

story and pictures by
Royden Lepp

Today is Barnabas Bear's
birthday.

Good morning, Barnabas!

"Thank you, Russell.

You remembered my birthday!"

"Please sit down, Russell,"
said Barnabas Bear.

"We'll have a cup of tea."

"There's Mr. Beaver,"
said Barnabas Bear.

"I wonder where he is going.
I wonder why he has a ladder."

"Would you like green tea
or black tea?" asked Barnabas.

"There's Peter Pig,"
said Barnabas.

"I wonder where he is going.
I wonder why he has crayons."

"Russell, could you please
pass the milk?"

"I wonder where Sara Skunk
is going with Gary Gator,"
said Barnabas.

"Why do they have balloons?"

"Would you like more tea,
Russell?" asked Barnabas.

"How about another cookie?"

"Where is everyone going?

Why do they need cupcakes?"

"Let's go to the farm,"
said Barnabas.

"Where is everyone?"

"Surprise! Happy birthday, Barnabas Bear!"

"Oh, thank you everyone,"
said Barnabas.

"Thank you, God,
for birthdays and cupcakes
and tea time with friends."